MW01351182

HOW TO SCARE A MONSTER!

WRITTEN BY
TOM HOLLAND & DUSTIN WARBURTON
ILLUSTRATED BY
LENNY K.

PUBLISHED BY
DEAD RABBIT FILMS LLC
215 ZELLY AVE.
MOORESTOWN, NJ 08057

FIRST EDITION
ISBN: 978-0-692-03341-8

HOW TO SCARE MONSTER
WRITTEN BY TOM HOLLAND AND DUSTIN WARBURTON
ILLUSTRATED BY LENNY K.
WWW.LEONARDKENYON.COM
SUPERVISING EDITOR
DAVID CHACKLER

IT WAS VERY LATE, BUT POOR LEONARD CHARLES VINCENT COULD NOT SLEEP. THERE WAS SOMETHING LURKING IN HIS CLOSET. IT SCRATCHED AND THUMPED, SCRAPED AND BUMPED.

HE PEERED OUT FROM BENEATH HIS COVERS . . .

THINK
THIN
CREAK
. . . AND THE
CLOSET DOOR SWUNG
SLOWLY OPEN.

THERE WAS
SOMETHING
INSIDE!

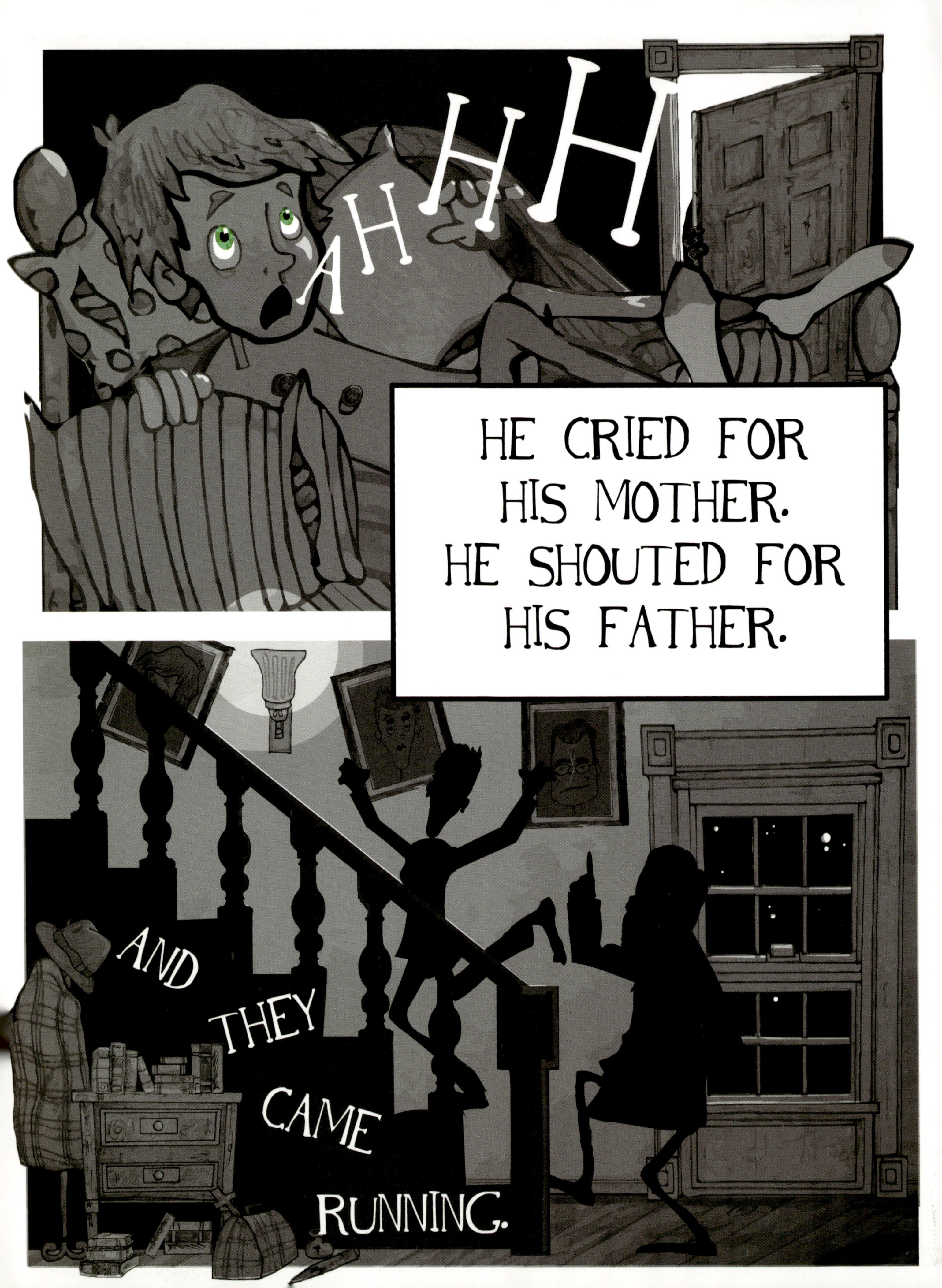
AHHHH
HE CRIED FOR HIS MOTHER. HE SHOUTED FOR HIS FATHER.
AND THEY CAME RUNNING.

friends only
"WHAT'S ALL THIS RACKET ABOUT?" MR. VINCENT BELLOWED.

"MU-MU-MONSTER!"
"IT'S NOT UNDER HERE," SAID MR. VINCENT, CHECKING THE BED.
"IT'S NOT BACK HERE EITHER," SAID MRS. VINCENT, INSPECTING THE NIGHTSTAND.
"LISTEN TO ME," CRIED LEONARD, "THE CLOSET!"

MR. VINCENT SWUNG THE CLOSET DOOR SHUT IN A HUFF. "THAT'S IT," HE SAID.

"YOUR MOTHER AND I HAVE HAD QUITE ENOUGH!"

"NO MORE COMICS. NO MORE SCARY MOVIES. THERE ARE NO SUCH THINGS AS TERRIBLE TALKING DOLLS OR GYPSY CURSES. POOR MR. SARANDON NEXT DOOR IS NOT A VAMPIRE, AND THERE ARE CERTAINLY, POSITIVELY, NO SUCH THINGS AS CLOSET MONSTERS!"

"BUT WHAT IF YOU'RE WRONG, DAD?" SAID LEONARD. "I SAW SOMETHING. I HEARD SOMETHING. I KNOW I DID."

JUST AS MR. VINCENT LOOKED AS THOUGH HE WOULD BLOW HIS TOP, HE SMILED KINDLY INSTEAD.

"YOU CAN'T BE AFRIAD OF EVERYTHING, SON. IF THERE REALLY IS A MONSTER, TRY SCARING IT BACK."

WITH THAT, MRS. VINCENT KISSED LEONARD ON HIS FOREHEAD, SWITCHED OFF HIS LIGHT, AND . . .

. . . TIPTOED OUT,
LEAVING HIS
BEDROOM DOOR
OPEN JUST A CRACK.

SCARE THE MONSTER BACK? THOUGHT LEONARD. IT ALMOST SOUNDED LIKE A GOOD IDEA UNTIL HIS BEDROOM DOOR SUDDENLY CLOSED TIGHT, WINKING OUT THE LAST OF HIS LIGHT.

AND THERE CAME
A
SCRAPING
BUMP
AND A
WHISPERING
THUMP
FROM HIS CLOSET
ONCE MORE.

HE CRIED FOR HIS MOTHER. HE YELLED FOR HIS FATHER.
MOM!
DAD!

THIS TIME THEY DID NOT COME.

SO SHIVERING AND SHAKING, LEONARD DOVE BACK DEEP BENEATH HIS COVERS.

BUMP.
THUMP.
SCRATCH.
SCRAPE,

WENT THE THING IN HIS CLOSET.

LEONARD SWITCHED ON HIS FLASHLIGHT AND COVERED HIS EARS. HE TRIED HUMMING A HAPPY SONG AND WISHING FOR MORNING, BUT IT DID NOT COME AND THE NOISES WENT ON AND ON.

SCRAPE.

BUMP.

THUMP.

SCRATCH.

WHAT SORT
OF MONSTER COULD
IT BE?
LEONARD WONDERED.

A ZOMBIE?
A VAMPIRE?
A WICKED
LITTLE DOLL?
OR WAS IT A GHOST?

ENOUGH, THOUGHT LEONARD. I CAN'T STAY UNDER THESE BLANKETS ALL NIGHT. MAYBE DAD WAS RIGHT.

SO HE SNUCK OUT OF HIS BED AND CREPT CAREFULLY ACROSS HIS ROOM.

SCARE IT BACK, HE THOUGHT. YES! THAT'S WHAT I'LL DO, BUT I'LL NEED TO BE PREPARED FIRST.
HE KNELT QUICKLY TO HIS TOY BOX AND . . .
YS
. . . HE FOUND A SHIELD, A CAPE, AND A HORNED HELMET.

READY AT LAST, LEONARD MADE HIS WAY SLOWLY AND QUIETLY TO THE CLOSET DOOR.

HE REACHED OUT,
YANKED THE DOOR BACK,
AND ROARED.

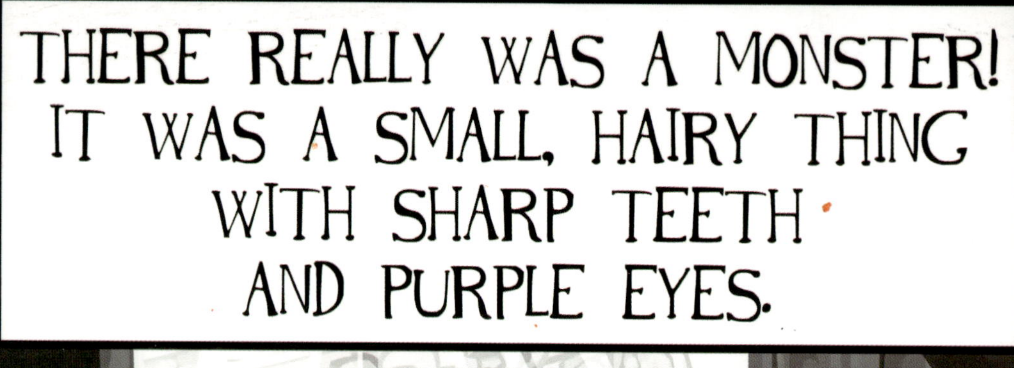

IT JUMPED BACK WITH A SQUELCHY SCREECH. "YOU NEARLY SCARED ME HALF TO DEATH!" IT CRIED.

"ME?" SAID LEONARD.

THE LITTLE MONSTER SIGHED. "I'M SORRY. IT'S JUST THAT MY DAD SAID THAT IF THERE REALLY WAS A HUMAN KEEPING ME UP AT NIGHT, I SHOULD TRY SCARING IT BACK."

LEONARD WAS ASTONISHED.

"SORRY ABOUT ALL OF THAT SCRATCHING AND THUMPING AND BUMPING AND SCRAPING," SAID THE LITTLE MONSTER. "BUT YOU'RE PRETTY NOISEY YOURSELF. YOU'RE ALWAYS SCREAMING AND SHOUTING AND HOLLERING AND WHOOPING. I HAVEN'T SLEPT IN MONTHS!"

"I GUESS I AM AFRAID OF EVERYTHING," SAID LEONARD.

"YOU LIVE IN MY CLOSET?" LEONARD ASKED.

"WELL," SAID THE LITTLE MONSTER, "JUST ON THE OTHER SIDE, BEYOND THE SHADOWS IS MY CLOSET. SO I GUESS IN A WAY YOU LIVE IN MINE, TOO."

"SO YOU'RE NOT GOING TO EAT ME OR ANYTHING?" LEONARD ASKED.

"YUCK!" THE LITTLE MONSTER HOOTED. "NO OFFENSE, BUT YOU'RE ONE OF THE UGLIEST THINGS I'VE EVER SEEN."

LEONARD HAD TO LAUGH.

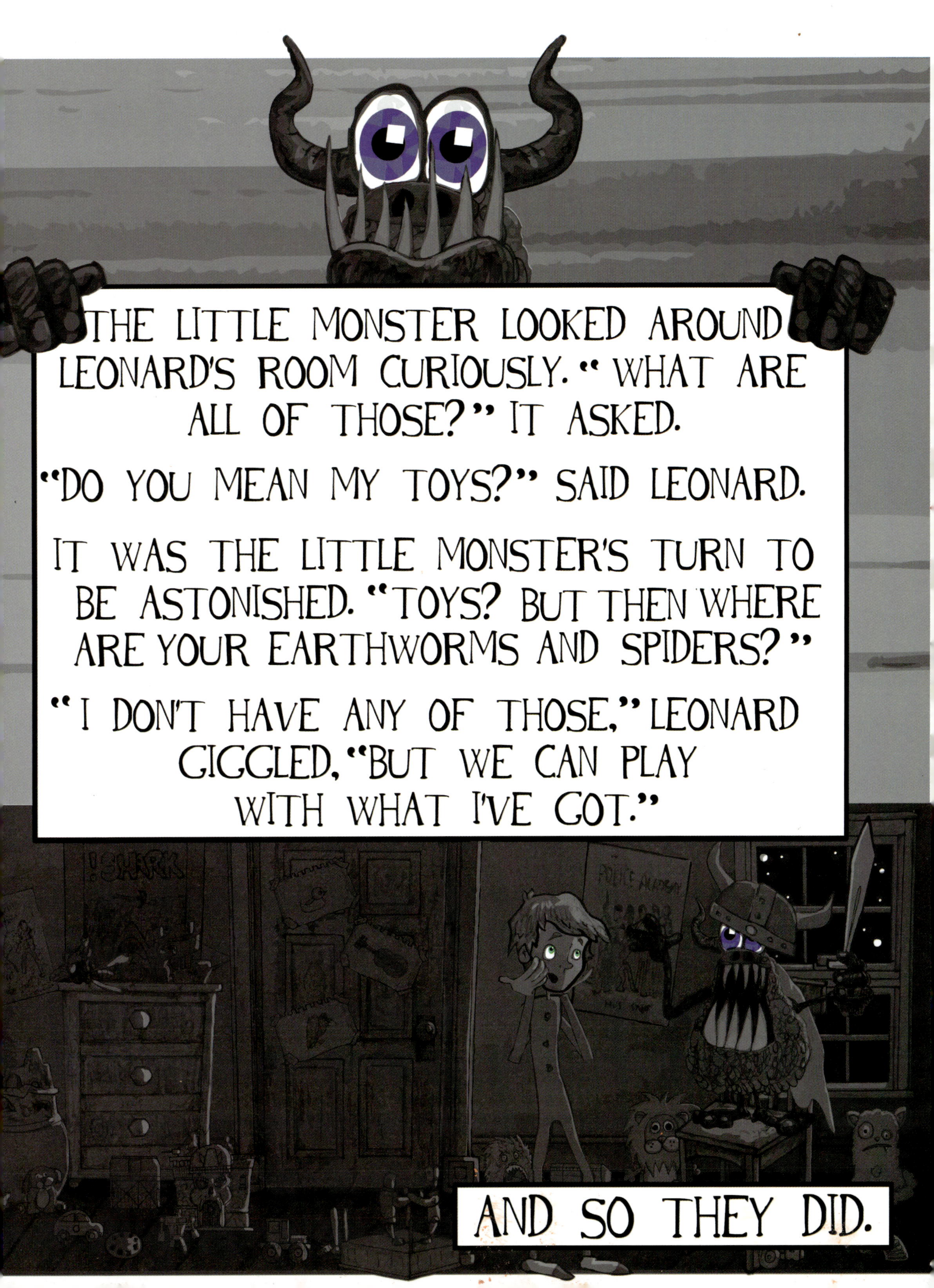
THE LITTLE MONSTER LOOKED AROUND LEONARD'S ROOM CURIOUSLY. "WHAT ARE ALL OF THOSE?" IT ASKED.
"DO YOU MEAN MY TOYS?" SAID LEONARD.
IT WAS THE LITTLE MONSTER'S TURN TO BE ASTONISHED. "TOYS? BUT THEN WHERE ARE YOUR EARTHWORMS AND SPIDERS?"
"I DON'T HAVE ANY OF THOSE," LEONARD GIGGLED, "BUT WE CAN PLAY WITH WHAT I'VE GOT."
AND SO THEY DID.

LEONARD AND THE LITTLE MONSTER PLAYED NEARLY ALL NIGHT UNTIL THEY BOTH GREW VERY TIRED AND IT WAS TIME FOR SLEEP. THE LITTLE MONSTER WRAPPED HIS ARMS AROUND LEONARD IN BIG A HUG.

"YOU MIGHT BE NOISEY AND ESPECIALLY UGLY," IT SAID, "BUT YOU'RE NOT ALL THAT SCARY AFTER ALL."

"EVERYTHING IS FINE, DAD," SAID LEONARD. AND FOR THE FIRST TIME IN A VERY LONG TIME, LEONARD CHARLES VINCENT MEANT IT.

THE LITTLE MONSTER SCRAMBLED BACK UP INTO HIS BED JUST AS HIS OWN FATHER APPEARED IN HIS DOORWAY.

"STILL WORRIED ABOUT CLOSET PEOPLE?" HE ASKED.

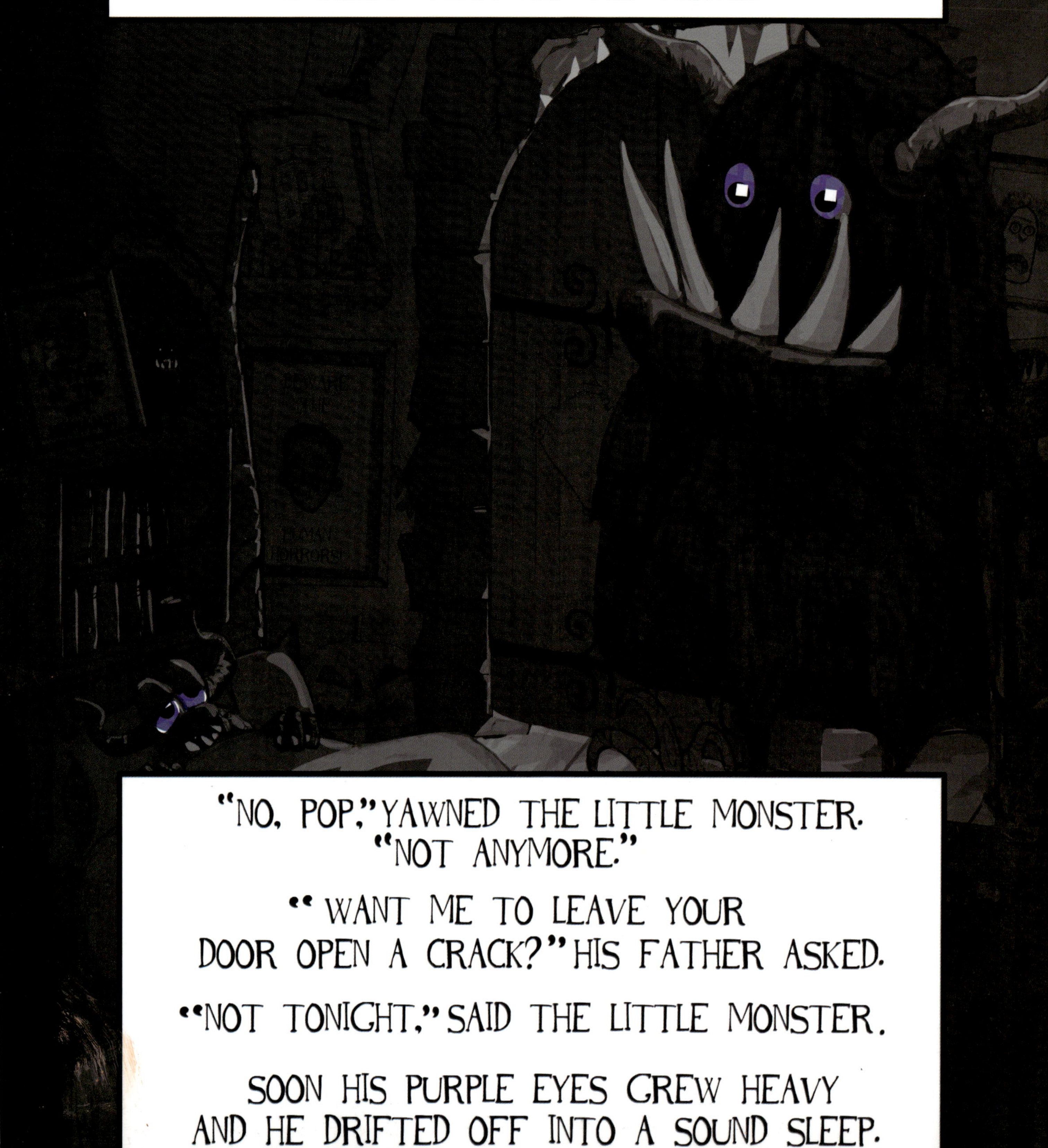